the idea of a

luctor," Mary answered. He would take me along for rides when I was just a toddler. I've always loved the sounds and rhythm of a train!" Then she ran and gave her grandfather a big hug.

Suddenly, a voice came from the outdoor speaker. "Shuttle number ninety-three on Track A will be delayed for fifteen minutes. We are sorry for the inconvenience."

Harry took off his bag and dropped it on the platform.

"Oh noooo!" Mary groaned.

Books in the Horrible Harry series

HORRIBLE HARRY
and the Birthday Girl

BY **SUZY KLINE**

PICTURES BY **AMY WUMMER**

PUFFIN BOOKS

PUFFIN BOOKS
An imprint of Penguin Random House LLC
375 Hudson Street
New York, New York 10014

First published in the United States of America by Viking,
an imprint of Penguin Random House LLC, 2016
Published by Puffin Books, an imprint of Penguin Random House LLC, 2017

THE LIBRARY OF CONGRESS HAS CATALOGED THE VIKING EDITION AS FOLLOWS:
Names: Kline, Suzy. Title: Horrible Harry and the birthday girl / by Suzy
Kline; illustrations by Amy Wummer. Description: New York :
Viking, published by Penguin Group, 2016. | Series: Horrible Harry ; 34 |
Summary: "It's Mary's birthday party. When things go horribly wrong will
Harry be able to save the day?"—Provided by publisher. Identifiers: LCCN
2015025667 | ISBN 978-0-451-47331-8 (hardback) Subjects: | CYAC:
Birthdays—Fiction. | Parties—Fiction. | Schools—Fiction. | Behavior—
Fiction. | BISAC: JUVENILE FICTION / Holidays & Celebrations /
Birthdays. | JUVENILE FICTION / Social Issues / Emotions & Feelings. |
JUVENILE FICTION / Transportation / Railroads & Trains. Classification:
LCC PZ7.K6797 Hfg 2016 | DDC [Fic]—dc23 LC record available at
https://protect-us.mimecast.com/s/RKomBxSepMbdC4

Puffin Books ISBN 9780147515124

Printed in the United States of America

1 3 5 7 9 10 8 6 4 2

DEDICATED TO
all the great readers at Crestline Elementary
School in Mountain View, Alabama.

Special appreciation to . . .

my dear editor, Leila Sales, and all her hard work; my helpful copy editor, Krista Ahlberg; Jennifer Smith, for having to deal with my five-hour delayed train; and my grandson Holden, who keeps his snow pants in his backpack longer than anyone I know.

HORRIBLE HARRY
and the Birthday Girl

Contents

Train Invitations

"Choo choooo!" Sidney ran into me like a train. "Doug!" he shouted. "Mary just invited *me* to her birthday party."

"All right, Sid!" I said, slapping him five. When I looked out at the playground of South School, I could see Mary handing invitations to Song Lee, Ida, ZuZu, and Dexter.

Sid flashed his invitation in my face. It had a train on it and the number 9.

"The party is this Saturday at noon. We're taking a train to University Park for a picnic lunch, concert, *and* outdoor play! I think Mary remembered that I don't get many invitations to parties, so she included me this time."

"Cool, Sid," I said, searching around for my friend Harry. I finally spotted him where the old fence used to be. He was looking at the two new portable classrooms that were being installed in the empty lot. When he saw us, he waved us over.

I waved back as we ran toward him.

"I'm invited to Mary's birthday party!" Sidney exclaimed. He was holding up his invitation like it was a trophy.

"Way to go, Sid," Harry said. Then he looked at me. "Mr. Beausoleil, our janitor,

told me our class can start using the nature area next week!"

Harry and I slapped each other ten. I knew that meant more to him than any birthday party.

"Harry! Doug!" Mary called out as she skipped over to us. "Here are your invitations to my party!"

"Neato, Mare!" Harry replied.

"Thanks!" I said.

"It's going to be the best birthday ever! I have the whole itinerary planned."

"I can't wait!" Sid said, then he asked, "What's an itinerary?"

"It's a schedule of when things happen," Mary explained.

Harry and I rolled our eyes. Mary was the most organized person in our third-grade class. It was annoying sometimes.

"Be sure to keep the invitation in your pocket," Mary ordered. "I don't want other kids feeling left out. I only could invite seven people." Then she glared at Sid. "So that means do *not* bring up the subject during morning conversation."

Sid looked disappointed. I think he wanted to keep waving that invitation around all day.

"I'll be watching you, Sidney LaFleur!" Mary said. "With my *eagle* eye!"

Harry's Gross Spring Cleaning

That morning, our teacher had written SPRING CLEANING on the whiteboard. It was still hard to get used to her new married name, Mrs. Flaubert, but most of our class remembered not to call her Miss Mackle. Except for one person.

"Miss Mackle," Sid blurted out.

"Mrs. Flaubert!" Mary corrected.

"Got it," Sid replied. Then he motioned for the teacher to come over to his desk.

"Yes, Sidney," Mrs. Flaubert said. "What is it?"

Sid lowered his voice, "I got an invi—"

Mary immediately shot him down. "Sidney LaFleur!"

Sid covered his mouth and quickly changed the subject. "Do we have to clean inside the desk too?"

"Absolutely!" the teacher replied. "Spring has been here now for three weeks, so it's time to do a thorough cleaning."

Mary gave Sid a thumbs-up.

All of us reached inside our desks and started pulling out the stuff inside.

Harry's desk was the worst. He made the mistake of tilting it forward to dump it out and accidently dropped the whole thing.

Blam! The loud noise caused everyone to look over.

"Harry!" Mary gasped. "That pile of stuff is horrible."

Sid pointed to something. "Is that a snake?"

"Just a rotten banana," Harry replied. "I forgot I left some old snacks in there."

There was also an apple with wrinkled skin that looked like it had been stepped on. There must have been forty pencil stubs, and a dozen purple library reminders all wadded up. Harry even had a small candy cane in there from Christmas. It was still wrapped in plastic. When he unwrapped it and took a bite, I cringed.

"Tastes fresh," Harry said.

"Harry Spooger," Mary said. "You

need to get organized. You have to sepa-
rate the good stuff from the garbage."

"Very little of this is garbage," Harry
objected. "You never know when it might
come in handy!"

"Really? A can of tomatoes?"

"Oh!" Harry replied. "I was looking for that. I wanted to donate it to the soup kitchen last week."

"Well, it's too late," Mary said. "The school food drive is over."

Song Lee turned to Harry. "I knew you'd bring something," she said with a smile.

Harry flashed a toothy grin.

Mary shook her head. "No wonder your library books are always overdue. When you're organized, Harry, and plan ahead, things run smoothly." Then she lowered her voice. "Like, this Saturday,

I have my birthday planned right down to the last minute. It will be the best party ever! And you know what would be the perfect gift you could give me?"

"Please tell me, Mare," Harry said. "I can't wait!"

Song Lee giggled. She knew Harry was teasing Mary.

"Come organized. Be on time, and don't forget my present."

"Got it, Mare! I will be very prepared. And just wait till you see what I plan to give you."

Mary beamed.

I couldn't wait to see Harry's gift either!

Hear a Choo Choo?

On Saturday, Harry's grandmother drove us to the train station. When we got out of her red truck, Harry slung a big backpack over his shoulder.

Mary's mother, Mrs. Berg, was standing in front of the train station, waving to us. A gray-haired man stood next to her, holding a blanket and a cake box. Mary was dressed in yellow, chatting with Song Lee, Ida, and Sidney.

As we walked up the ramp to the train tracks, I asked Harry about his bag. "How come you brought that big thing with you? We're not going to school. It's a party!"

Harry stopped and adjusted his shoulder strap. "I came organized. That's what Mary wanted. I have everything inside that we might need on the train or in the park for the concert and play."

"And your gift is inside?"

"Yes! But there is more than one. I have all kinds of stuff in here for her! Grandma gave me ten dollars to spend at the dollar store. I just added one item from our bathroom. And a homemade card, of course." Then Harry flashed his white teeth.

I was beginning to get worried about Harry's presents. One item from his *bathroom*?

"Ooookay . . ." I replied, switching my heavy gift bag to my other hand. "I wish mine didn't weigh so much."

"Welcome, boys!" Mrs. Berg sang out. "So glad you're here. This is Mary's grandfather. We call him Papa."

"Hey, guys!" Papa said, holding up his right hand.

Harry and I slapped it five, then joined ZuZu and Dexter at the top of the ramp. We were the last to arrive.

"Ready to rock and roll?" Dexter asked. "I brought my guitar."

Papa looked over and gave us a V for Victory sign. "I should have brought my violin. We could have done a duet!"

he commented. Then he pantomimed playing one.

Mary interrupted our conversation. "We don't have time for anything extra, guys. The itinerary is already set." Then she pulled out a piece of paper from her matching yellow purse and checked it. "The train is due any minute now. We have to go wait for it on the platform."

I locked eyes with Dexter and then rolled them around a few times. Mary was being a real party pooper.

When we gathered on the platform, I noticed a gray-haired lady waiting there with her two suitcases. Another older woman was holding a long-strapped duffel bag. A man in a suit with a briefcase was reading the newspaper. Six college students stood nearby. They were joking around, listening to their earphones, or reading books.

"The shuttle to University Park is just a local train," Mary announced. "It only has three cars. As soon as it gets to its destination, it turns around and goes back. Most people transfer at University Station if they want to go farther."

Mrs. Berg set her red cooler down. "We should hear the train coming any minute now!"

Mary and the girls jumped up and down.

"I love riding on the train!" Mary said. "Even though University Park is just two stops away, it's a fun eighteen-minute ride through the woodlands."

"I can't wait," Song Lee replied. "I've never gone to a train party before."

"How did you come up with the idea of a train party?" ZuZu asked.

"Papa used to be a conductor," Mary answered. "He would take me along for rides when I was just a toddler. I've always loved the sounds and rhythm of a train!" Then she ran and gave her grandfather a big hug.

Suddenly, a voice came from the outdoor speaker. "Shuttle number ninety-

three on Track A will be delayed for
fifteen minutes. We are sorry for the
inconvenience."

Harry took off his bag and dropped it
on the platform.

"Oh noooo!" Mary groaned.

The Platform Drama

Mrs. Berg sat down on her red cooler and looked at her watch.

All the guests put their presents on the platform.

"Train delays happen," Papa said. "I know! But hey, now we have time for Dexter's guitar."

Mary plopped down on Harry's bag while everyone else gathered around to listen. Dexter started strumming an old Elvis tune, "All Shook Up." Three of the college students started moving and keeping time to the beat. The two older ladies did the hand jive and swayed their hips.

"Everybody, let's rock!" Sid called out.

Papa reached for Mrs. Berg's hand, but she shook her head. When he went over to Mary, she said, "No thanks. I don't feel like twirling."

"I do!" Ida exclaimed as she grabbed Sidney's hand.

Mary looked up at Harry. "What do you have in this bag, anyway? It's nice and soft."

"Special stuff for you. I came organized," Harry replied. "Like you asked."

"I came organized too," Mary said, putting her list back into her purse. "What good is that now?"

"The train is just fifteen minutes late," I said.

"Yes, but *that* means we'll miss half the concert! And we'll have to rush to finish lunch and cake and presents before the play on the green starts."

"The play isn't until two o'clock," her mother chimed in, trying to be hopeful.

"Want to see what's inside my backpack?" Harry asked, changing the subject.

"No," Mary said. "I'm too comfortable sitting on it."

"I'm having fun!" Sid said, spinning Ida around to the beat of the music.

Song Lee sat down next to Mary on a corner of Harry's bag. "I'm sorry you're sad," she said. "But the late train is not your fault."

Mary nodded.

"It still is going to be the best party!" Song Lee added.

"Everybody rock!" Dexter sang out, strumming a different Elvis tune.

Now Ida was dancing with ZuZu!

When Mary jumped up and started twirling around with Song Lee, Harry and I clapped. "Go, Mare!" we called out.

Then right in the middle of all that

rock-and-rolling came another announcement over the loudspeaker.

Dexter stopped playing. Everyone froze.

"Train number ninety-three on Track A will be arriving at 12:19 p.m."

Mary immediately let go of Song Lee's hands. "That makes it a nineteen-minute delay!" she said, stomping her feet. "*Not* fifteen minutes."

"It's just a few minutes longer than they said before," Sid replied.

"It's *four* minutes longer!" Mary corrected. "'A few' is just two or three! Why does this have to happen to *my* party?"

Mrs. Berg got up and put her arm around Mary. "We have plenty of time, dear. We can always eat lunch and cake while we're watching the play. It would be like a dinner theater!"

"Yes," Papa agreed. "It will be even more fun that way."

Mary wasn't buying it. She sank back down on Harry's bag and covered her ears.

I could tell the only music Mary wanted to hear right now was the sound of a train.

Harry's Bag of Gifts

*W*hooo! *Whooo!*

Finally the train whistled as it rounded the corner and headed for Track A. The loudspeaker confirmed its arrival as it *shhhhhh-shhhhhhh*ed to a screeching stop.

"All right!" Mary shouted, jumping to her feet. "Let's go!"

The conductor hopped down to the platform to help the elderly ladies on first. Harry and I grabbed our stuff and got at the end of the line.

"What *do* you have in that bag, Harry?" ZuZu asked.

"A bunch of birthday treats for Mary," Harry answered.

I wasn't so sure that everything he'd brought was going to be a treat.

The conductor grabbed the handle of the red cooler and hoisted it up through the doorway. Then he offered Mrs. Berg an arm. She climbed up the steps and led our party onto the train.

Mrs. Berg led us into one long car that was half-filled with people. "These are the coach class seats," she said.

"What's that mean?" Sid asked ZuZu.

"They're the cheapest seats," he said.

The six college students and the elderly

ladies looked for places to sit in that car. I noticed a toddler standing on her mom's lap, patting the window. Several people were reading. Lots of people were talking. When we got to the end of the aisle, we passed by two long bathrooms, each with a sliding door.

Harry stepped inside one immediately. When he locked the door, the word OCCUPIED lit up in front. "I wish I had one of those signs at my house," I said to Sidney. "My brother Baxter is always banging on the door screaming, 'Anybody in there?'"

"We're sitting in the café car," Mrs. Berg said. When she tapped the door at the back of the car, it sprang open right away. There was a little platform separating the cars. We stepped on it and waited for Mary's mom to touch the next door. "Let's find two empty tables that are across the aisle from each other," she continued.

As soon as Harry joined us, Mrs. Berg rapped on the door behind her. It sprang open like the other one, and we stepped inside.

Mary bulldozed her way to the front and picked out two tables in the middle. I noticed just a couple of people were

in the café car—one guy drinking coffee and doing a crossword puzzle, and a woman typing something on her laptop.

"The first car is always the business class," Mrs. Berg said.

"You get a free bottle of water and a newspaper," Mary added. "But it costs more to sit there."

The man in the suit was heading for that section.

So was Harry.

He followed that man down the aisle

into the business class car. Papa took off after him. "Wait, Harry," he called out.

Two minutes later they both returned. Harry scooted into the booth next to me.

"They have two bathrooms in that car too," he said. "Right next to the entrance door. And it's very quiet. Everyone is sitting up and working on something."

"Anything else, Harry?" I asked. I was curious about that first car and why it cost more money.

"The seats are really comfortable. I tried one out. Lots of padding."

Chooo-chooo, chooo-chooo. . . . We could hear the train leaving the station as it jerked forward and then bounced back and forth. I loved the swaying.

It was like being in a rocking chair. I also liked the *clickety-clack* of the steel wheels on the track.

"Here we go, guys!" Papa called out. "Enjoy the ride!"

Mary clapped her hands. She seemed  in a much better mood now that we were moving. Dexter rested his guitar case against the wall. We set the presents down on the floor under the table.

A loudspeaker near us turned on, and a voice came through it saying, "Next stop is Marion. And then University Park at 12:40 p.m."

"Actually, having a dinner theater in the park sounds like fun," Mary reasoned. Then she looked under the table. "Gee, thanks for bringing all the presents, guys. I can't wait to open them."

As the train chugged along, Harry took out his bag. "I brought some stuff that we could use on our trip," he said, looking at Mary. He had to take a big item out first. We all watched him as we bounced and jiggled to the left and right.

"Snow pants!" Mary scoffed. "Are those *still* in your backpack from winter?"

"You never know, Mare. They might be handy," Harry explained.

Mary rolled her eyes. "We don't have to wear those anymore for outdoor recess, Harry. There are no more snowbanks. I thought you were getting organized!"

Papa and Mrs. Berg chuckled.

Next Harry pulled out a bag of lollipops, a bunch of ribbons, two packs of
chewing gum, a magnifying glass, and
toothpaste.

So that was the one item from the
bathroom: toothpaste! I was relieved it
wasn't a roll of toilet paper.

"I got five spools of different-colored
ribbon from the dollar store and cut
them into streamers for your birthday,
Mare."

"Can I have a lollipop?" Sid asked.

"No!" Mary scolded. "You don't want
to spoil your lunch. Now, how is that
stuff useful, Harry?"

"Well, Elmer Elevator used these
things in *My Father's Dragon* when he
had his adventure on Wild Island."

"That's one of your favorite books, isn't it, Harry?" Song Lee said.

Mary folded her arms. "This is not Wild Island, Harry! There are no crocodiles or baby dragons around here."

"There are no snow pants in Elmer's bag either," ZuZu said. "I read that book too."

"Right," Harry said with a grin. "The snow pants were my idea! But everything else is what Elmer used to save the day. You never know when you might have an adventure. I'm prepared for one!"

Suddenly, the train started going slower and slower until . . . *shhhh, shhh, shhh!* It came to a halt. *Shhhhhhhh!*

"Are we at Marion already?" ZuZu asked.

It was quiet for two long minutes.

Suddenly a voice came over the loud-speaker. "We are very sorry to inform you that we are having some mechanical difficulties. We'll let you know when it's safe to resume travel. It could be as much as an hour's delay. Again, we apologize for this inconvenience."

"Ohhh!" Mary dropped her head on the table and pounded her fist. "No fair! My party is a disaster!"

Party Disaster!

During Mary's outburst, the guy with the coffee and crossword puzzle got up and left for the coach class car.

The woman with the laptop headed for the business class car.

Mary's tantrum had cleared out the café! It was just us now. We had the whole car to ourselves. I thought that was neat!

Harry and I looked out the window

while Mary pounded the table. We were stuck in the middle of a forest all right.

"We've got a real adventure!" Harry exclaimed. "This is going to be so cool!"

Mary looked up briefly, took a breath, and then rested her head on the table again.

Mrs. Berg rolled out the red cooler and started passing out birthday napkins and birthday plates. "Harry is right," she agreed. "The party is going to be even more fun! We can enjoy lunch now on the train in our own private café car, and *then* look forward to the play on the green in University Park. Who's hungry?"

Mary closed her eyes and plugged her ears.

"I am!" lots of us blurted out.

Mrs. Berg set plastic bowls down on the table. Then she put a plate of sandwiches in the middle. The crusts were cut off and they were all in the shape of triangles. "There's egg, tuna with celery, chicken salad, and ham and cheese. Help yourself to the potato salad and chips," she said. "And Island Punch."

Song Lee tapped Mary on the shoulder. Very gently, she removed one hand from Mary's ear and whispered, "Isn't Island Punch your favorite drink?"

Mary suddenly sat up and opened her eyes. *"Island Punch!"* she repeated. The

name of the drink changed her mood completely. "It's the only time I get to drink it. On my birthday! I almost forgot! Thanks, Song Lee!" She gave her friend a big hug. Song Lee hugged her back.

We watched Mrs. Berg pour the punch into our plastic cups.

Mary stared at the red drink like it was liquid rubies. "Mom says it has too much sugar, but she lets me choose whatever I want to eat and drink on my birthday."

While the rest of us reached for the sandwiches, Mary guzzled down her punch. She had

a red mustache, but no one said anything.

When I reached for a second ham and cheese sandwich, I noticed that Mary had poured herself another glass of punch.

Her mother got up and had a word with her.

"No more," Mrs. Berg whispered. "We have milk too."

Mary made a face.

"Too bad we're going to miss the concert," Sid said.

Ida jabbed Sid in the side. "Shhh!" she snapped.

Sid's words made Mary get grumpy again. "Don't remind me!" she moaned. "So what do we do after lunch? We're stuck here."

Harry piped up with an idea. "We have a parade!"

"What kind of a parade?" Mary asked.

"A birthday parade, of course. And you are the main event, Mare!"

Mary was listening closely.

Harry continued, "We'll march down the train aisle, waving ribbons, passing out lollipops and sticks of gum to the passengers, *and* singing the happy birthday song. Dex, can you play it on your guitar?"

"Of course I can," he replied.

Mary wasn't frowning anymore. "Where do I march?"

"At the end! You're like the bride in the wedding. Everyone waits to see you come down the aisle. The best is saved for last! You will get nine ribbons. Everyone else gets two."

Mary broke out in a smile. She loved being the center of attention.

Mrs. Berg clapped her hands. "A delightful idea, Harry! And after the parade, we'll have cake in the café car!"

Now everyone clapped and cheered.

Papa came over and put two thumbs up. "You kids will make your own concert!" Then he handed Dexter his guitar and patted him on the shoulder.

Harry started passing out the ribbons, gum, and lollipops. "If any of you want to brush your teeth with your finger, I've got toothpaste. You can rinse out your mouth in the bathroom. Just don't drink the water," he said.

There were no takers.

When Mary reached for the red drink again, Mrs. Berg grabbed it. "I said no more," she whispered firmly, and set a half-pint of milk in front of her.

As soon as Dexter began strumming a few notes, Harry stood up. "Are you guys ready to go?"

"I am," Mrs. Berg said. "I'm going to the back of the coach class car to videotape the parade!"

"I'm coming too," Papa added, chucking a chip in his mouth. They both hurried ahead.

I went to the end of the line. "I'll join you in a minute," Mary said. "You guys go ahead. I want to put ribbons in my hair."

"Good idea," Ida said. "That way every-one will know you're the birthday girl!"

"Okay, Dexter, let it rip!" Harry ordered.

Dexter began playing the birth-day song as we practiced marching in place. "Left, left, left right, left!" Harry chanted. Then he switched directions.

"About-face!" When Harry turned around and faced the opposite direc-tion, we did too.

"Left, left, left right, left! About-face!"
We were ready!

Harry led us down the aisle, tapped on the sliding door, and stepped onto the platform. Then he touched the door in front of him, waited for it to spring open, and proceeded to march into the coach class car.

I waited for Mary on the platform in between the cars. When the sliding door closed in front of me, I turned around to look through the little window into the café car. Mary was not putting ribbons in her hair.

She was doing something that made my jaw drop and my eyes bulge.

Through the Café Car Window

Mary was pouring herself *another* cup of that red drink after her mom told her no more! *Oh boy,* I thought, *I'd better join the parade fast.* I didn't want her to know I saw her. I'm no tattletale!

After I hurried through the sliding door, I joined the parade marching down the aisle in the coach class car. The two elderly ladies were standing up and smiling. Sidney and Ida were

circling their ribbons in the air like
lassos. We handed out lollipops and
sticks of gum. As Dexter strummed the
song, we all sang the familiar verse.

The college students loved the gum.
They started chewing it right away.

When Mary didn't come through the
sliding door, Harry looked back at me.
"Where's the birthday girl?" he asked.

"She'll be here in a minute," I said.
"Keep singing!"

That minute seemed like an hour.

"Keep marching!" I said.

Harry led the parade to the end of the coach class car. Mrs. Berg and Papa were waiting for us. Mary's mom was videotaping the parade with her phone.

After we finished singing the birthday song, Harry announced, "The birthday girl is about to make her entrance!" The college students had put their earphones and books away. They were standing on their knees on their seats, watching us pass by.

Harry dashed over to me at the end of the line. "Let's go check on Mare," he whispered. Then he looked back at everyone. "And now Dexter will play a popular Elvis tune!"

As Harry and I hurried down the

aisle, the elderly ladies called out, "Where's the birthday girl?"

"Coming!" I said. "She's putting ribbons in her hair."

The ladies clapped their hands.

The toddler was licking her lollipop.

Harry and I raced out the door and into the café car.

When we got there, it was empty!

"Where's Mary?" Harry exclaimed. "She's not here!"

Where's Mary?

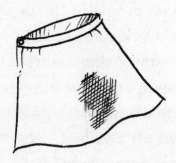

After we checked the café car, we passed through the sliding door into the business class car. "The bathrooms are right here," Harry said. "Let's check!"

One was open, so we looked inside.

"Not here," Harry said.

He knocked on the door of the other bathroom, which had the word OCCUPIED in capitals just above the handle.

"Mare?" Harry whispered. We didn't want to call attention to what we were doing. The people in the business class car were working so quietly.

Very slowly the sliding door opened just enough to show Mary's face. Her eyes were all red.

"I had an accident," she whispered, "and I need your help."

Harry and I exchanged a quick look.

"Nooo," Mary groaned. "I did not have a bathroom accident!" Then she opened up the sliding bathroom door wider to show her yellow skirt. She had spilled that red drink all over the front of it!

"Mom will kill me! She told me not to have a third cup. She'll know when she sees me. Can I borrow those snow pants, Harry?"

Harry didn't even answer. He took
off like a flash and retrieved the pants
for her.

"Harry Spooger, you saved my life!"

Mary quickly closed the door and
then opened it a little again. "Put this
skirt in your bag!" she told Harry. Then

she slammed the door shut to finish changing.

I stepped out onto the platform and looked through the window into the café car.

Harry was running down the aisle. When he got to his black bag, he dropped the skirt in, but just as he was zipping it up, Mrs. Berg burst into the café car.

She had a quick word with Harry, then they both stormed down the aisle toward me.

Oh man! I thought. *This could be trouble!*

The Birthday Girl

Mrs. Berg had a worried look.

"She's in there," I volunteered, pointing to the bathroom.

"Everything okay?" she asked.

Mary stepped out of the bathroom to answer her mother's question. "I'm fine!" Mary said. She had tied the nine ribbons in her hair. "Like my birthday hairdo?"

"Why did you put on Harry's snow pants?" her mom asked.

Mary looked at Harry, and he answered for her. "They're really comfortable."

"Ohhh!" Mrs. Berg replied. "Don't worry about it, dear. Those things happen. Go join our birthday parade! Everyone will be looking at your colorful ribbons."

Apparently Harry and I weren't the only ones who thought Mary had had a bathroom accident.

We took off to join the marchers. Dexter was entertaining everyone with his Elvis songs on the guitar. When Mary appeared, everyone cheered. "The birthday girl is here!" Harry shouted.

Mary waved. We all repeated the birthday song. This time, the passengers joined in.

"I love your ribbon hairdo!" Song Lee said.

Mary beamed.

"Why are you wearing Harry's pants?" ZuZu asked.

"They're my marching pants," Mary answered confidently. Apparently she'd had enough thinking time to come up with a better answer.

"Cool!" Sid replied.

Mary walked all the way to the front, smiling right at her grandfather. We marched in place until the song was over. Then Harry rushed to the back of the line where I was and called out, "About-face!"

Everyone turned around.

"Forward march!" Harry barked, pointing ahead with his last lollipop.

Harry and I led the group down the aisle, singing the second verse of "Happy Birthday." "Are you one? Are you two? Are you three? Are you four?" until we got to nine. The elderly ladies were counting with us on their fingers. The toddler was reaching for Harry's lollipop. He handed it to her when he passed by.

The guy who was working on that crossword puzzle raised his coffee cup to toast the birthday girl.

Mary was like the queen of the parade. She greeted everyone graciously and even shook their hands. Passengers commented on her ribbon hairdo and said she was beautiful. Mary was absolutely glowing!

Sid was raising his knees high in the air as he marched down the aisle. ZuZu had perfect posture. His shoulders were back and his head was held high. He looked like one of those British soldiers

that guard the palace. He didn't even blink!

When we finally got back to the café car, Sidney blurted out, "This is the best party ever!"

"I wanted to keep marching," ZuZu added.

Mary twirled around and giggled.

"How about some cake?" Mrs. Berg asked.

"Yes!" we all shouted.

While Papa passed out cupcakes with M&M'S on top to stand for Mary, Mrs. Berg came around with the drinks. "Milk or Island Punch?" Just about everyone chose the punch. When she came to Mary, she asked, "Would you like another cup too, honey?"

Mary looked up. She seemed more serious now, but she didn't say anything.

Suddenly, Harry called her name.

"Mare?" he said. He had just stepped out of the bathroom and was closing the sliding door to the business class car.

Mary got up and met him halfway down the aisle.

I couldn't tell what they were saying, but it was a very short conversation.

When Mary returned to her seat, she stared at the red drink in her cup. Her mom had poured her another serving.

I was dying to ask Harry what they had talked about, but I kept my eyes on Mary instead.

Everyone else was admiring their cupcakes with the pink icing. Harry was already stuffing his face with one!

Mary motioned for her mom to come over. Mrs. Berg did. "Yes, dear?"

"I've . . . already . . . had a third cup, although most of it . . . splashed on my skirt," Mary admitted. "So sorry, Mom."

Mrs. Berg lowered her voice to a whisper. "I'm glad you told me the truth."

"I rinsed out the punch stain right away with cold water just like you taught me," Mary added.

Mrs. Berg smiled. "Good girl. I'm so relieved it wasn't a bathroom accident."

"I'm really sorry I didn't tell you the truth right away, Mom. I was afraid you might hate me."

"Oh, Mary! Nothing could change the way I feel about you. I will always love you. You can tell me anything."

"I know that now," she said. When

Mary gave her mom a big hug, her mom hugged her back longer.

I turned and whispered in Harry's ear. "What did you and Mary talk about that changed her mind?"

Harry shrugged. He had pink icing all over his hands. "I just told her what her mom told me when she came looking for her earlier."

"What was that?"

"She said Mary was the love of her life."

"What did Mary say?"

"She said, 'Really?' I was afraid

Mary might get grumpy again since the parade was over, so I thought she needed to hear something nice."

I handed Harry a napkin, then gave him two thumbs up. "Way to go!" I said. "You saved the party in more ways than one."

When Harry smiled, his teeth were pink!

Eweyee! I thought.

Epilogue

We made it to University Park just in time to see the play on the outdoor stage. We had missed the concert, but that was okay. We all sat down on the large blanket and enjoyed *The Music Man* together. All of us got up and marched around the blanket when "Seventy-Six Trombones" was played!

After the musical, Papa bought

everyone ice cream from the vendor at the park, and we opened presents on the green.

Dexter gave Mary a CD of Elvis's biggest hits.

Song Lee gave her a necklace that she had strung herself with colorful buttons.

Ida gave her a diary with a key.

I gave her a big, heavy dictionary.

Sid gave her a small gold box of French chocolates. He said they were bonbons. (Sid is big on French things.)

ZuZu gave her a stuffed animal. It looked just like JouJou, his pet tortoise-shell guinea pig who visited our class last year.

Harry had made a homemade card with drawings of nine insects and bugs crawling around the words *Happy Birthday.* When Mary opened it up, she smiled, then read Harry's words inside: *Hope you enjoy the birthday treats I brought you.*

"Well, thank you, Harry," Mary said. "The ribbons were lots of fun for our parade, *and* my birthday hairdo! I liked the lollipops too. They were a hit with the passengers. And thanks for letting me wear these pants. They sure came in handy . . . for *marching*!"

She winked at Harry and me and her mom when she said that last part. It was our secret.

"I knew those snow pants could be useful," Harry replied. "That's why I don't throw anything out! Not even this ice cream stick." Then he dropped it into his bag and zipped it up.

"Eweyee!" Mary moaned. "You're gross, Harry Spooger."

And that is one thing Mary and I can agree on!